Kitty Neale was raised in South London and this working class area became the inspiration for her novels. In the 1980s she moved to Surrey with her husband and two children, but in 1998 there was a catalyst in her life when her son died, aged just 27. After joining other bereaved parents in a support group, Kitty was inspired to take up writing and her books have been *Sunday Times* bestsellers.

...ty now lives in Spain with her husband.

...find out more about Kitty go to
www.kittyneale.co.uk

By the same author:

Nobody's Girl
Sins of the Father
Desperate Measures
Lost and Found
Forgotten Child
Lost Angel
Mother's Ruin

KITTY NEALE

Family Betrayal

AVON

This novel is entirely a work of fiction.
The names, characters and incidents portrayed in it are
the work of the author's imagination. Any resemblance to
actual persons, living or dead, events or localities is
entirely coincidental.

AVON

A division of HarperCollins*Publishers*
77–85 Fulham Palace Road,
London W6 8JB

www.harpercollins.co.uk

This paperback edition 2011

1

First published in Great Britain by
HarperCollins*Publishers* 2008

A catalogue record for this book is
available from the British Library

ISBN-13: 978-1-84756-350-7

Typeset in Minion by Palimpsest Book Production Limited,
Grangemouth, Stirlingshire

Printed and bound in Great Britain by
Clays Ltd, St Ives Plc

Mixed Sources
Product group from well-managed
forests and other controlled sources
www.fsc.org Cert no. SW-COC-1806
© 1996 Forest Stewardship Council

FSC is a non-profit international organisation established to promote the
responsible management of the world's forests. Products carrying the FSC
label are independently certified to assure consumers that they come
from forests that are managed to meet the social, economic and
ecological needs of present and future generations.

Find out more about HarperCollins and the environment at
www.harpercollins.co.uk/green

My thanks to my editor Maxine Hitchcock and her team at Avon/HarperCollins. It has been a difficult year for me, but they were always there to offer their kind support. Thanks also to my wonderful husband Jim and daughter Samantha, two precious people who keep me smiling.

This book is dedicated to my dear cousin, Roberta Carter, a woman whose courage in the face of illness has been an inspiration.

Prologue

Nervously, the young woman approached Drapers Alley. She had been told all but one of the houses were empty, yet still her heart thudded with fear.

Had her informant lied? It was possible. There was still venom – spite aimed at her family – locals who wanted to see her, and them, brought low. For a moment she froze, wanting to turn and flee, but she had to risk it – had to tell her mother the awful truth.

Taking a deep breath to calm her nerves, she entered the narrow passageway, skirting the iron bollard that barred all traffic but that on two wheels. The sign was still on the wall, the alley's name, but now her eyes widened. Her father had ruled here – followed by her brothers after his death – and no one had dared enter their domain without permission. She'd been gone for only just over six months but already the D in 'Drapers' had been crudely painted out so that it read 'Rapers Alley'.

1

Yes, rape may have been one of their sins, it was certainly possible, yet worse had been done – much worse.

The fact that the name had been defaced was all the proof she needed that her brothers had gone, and the tension at last left her body. To one side of the alley a towering, dirty factory wall cut out light, the atmosphere it created grim with foreboding. Above the high wall the upper floors of the factory were visible, lined with a myriad mean, grimy windows. Though it had closed many years ago, it was a building that had dominated her life from childhood, and visible as soon as she stepped outside the front door. She hated it, had longed to see grass and trees, but unlike her nephews, she hadn't been allowed the pleasure of playing in the local park.

Her eyes avoided the factory building and the horror of what would be found inside. Instead she looked to the left and for a moment paused to take in the small row of six flat-fronted workers' houses. They appeared smaller, shabby with neglect, yet the first in the row, number one, stood out as different. This was her parents' home – a home she'd been forced to flee in fear of her life.

As she crossed the narrow cobbled alley, her gaze fixed on the house, a ray of spring sunlight pierced the gloom. Like her, it had dared to penetrate the alley and it momentarily illuminated her mother's window. Was it a good omen? Did it mean she'd be safe? God, she hoped so.

The brass door knocker and letter box gleamed, but instead of smiling, her lips thinned. Now that her mother was alone, she'd expected her to change – to give up her obsession with housework. Her mother had dusted, polished, swept and scrubbed every hour of the day, excluding any opportunity to show her children an ounce of affection.

For a moment she hesitated outside the street door. What if she'd been lied to? What if her mother wasn't alone? Come on, she told herself, show a bit of spunk. You've come this far and nobody would have dared to call it Rapers Alley if they were still around.

Her hand lifted slowly to the small lion's-head knocker and, after rapping three times, she involuntarily stepped back a pace.

The door slowly opened. 'Is it really you?'

'Yes, Mum,' she said, and seeing the smile of welcome on her mother's face, her eyes filled with tears as she stepped inside. What she had to tell her mother would break her heart.

Chapter One

Drapers Alley, South London, May 1962

Dan Draper was fond of relating the tale of how he'd found the alley, and on Saturday morning he was repeating it again as he sat facing his youngest son. Dan's pug-nosed face was animated, his huge tattooed arms resting on the table.

At twenty-four years old, Chris Draper was a replica of his father. He shared his light brown hair and grey eyes, along with his tall, beefy build, both of them standing at six foot. But so far his nose remained unbroken and his good looks were intact.

'Yes, you've told me, Dad,' Chris said wearily as he cut vigorously into his rasher of crispy bacon.

Dan carried on as though he hadn't noticed the interruption. 'I'd had a few beers too many and my bladder was bursting. It was sheer chance that I cut into this alley for a slash. You could have knocked me down with a feather when I saw the name. Blimey, it was like fate. Not only that, I saw the potential straight away. With narrow entrances at both ends, cut in half by the bollards, the only thing that can get through is a bike.'

'Yeah, I know.'

'This alley is as good as a fortress.'

Chris nodded, hardly listening as his father rambled on. He looked at his mother, Joan, her hands busy as always polishing the brass ornaments. She appeared distant, unreachable, but Chris was used to this. In his childhood it had upset him, but he was a man now, and he didn't need displays of motherly affection, or so he told himself. She was a tiny woman, two inches less than five foot tall and as usual, she aroused his protective instincts.

'Are you all right, Mum?' he asked.

It was his father who answered. 'Of course she's all right. Why shouldn't she be? Now then, where was I? Oh, yes, there was only one house empty in the alley at the time and I had to tip up a back-hander to the council to get it. Gawd, despite homes being in short supply, you should have seen your mother's face when she saw it. We'd been living in a flat with a shared bog so I thought she'd be excited, but instead she nearly had a fit. All right, this place is small and it was a bit of a squash to fit us all in, but at least we had it to ourselves.'

'Yeah, I was only a kid, but I can remember when

we moved from that dump of a place around the corner.'

'A year later your mother dropped a girl, making it a tighter squeeze. After giving me five sons it was a bit of a shock.'

Chris heard his mother's tut of displeasure but she said nothing, having given up remarking on her husband's coarseness years ago. He looked around the immaculate room, knowing that the outside of the house bore no relation to the interior. In their line of business it would give the game away to flaunt their wealth, yet even so, inside there was every comfort that the business books could account for. Against one wall sat a deep red velvet sofa, the gold tassels along the bottom hanging just short of the Wilton rug. To one side of the small Victorian fireplace there was a matching chair, but Chris's eyes were drawn to the radiogram, which, thanks to his mother's overzealous cleaning, looked as shiny and new as the day his father had bought it. With a small table and four chairs in the centre, the room was crammed to the rafters, yet from the brass fender to the ornaments, everything was sparkling. When they had first moved in there hadn't been a bathroom, just an outside loo, but his father had solved that problem by building an extension, one that took up half the yard. Chris smiled. He hero-worshipped his father and admired how clever he had been when installing the bathroom – one with a secret that only the male members of the family were aware of.

'Oi! Are you listening to me or am I talking to myself?'

'I'm listening, Dad.'

'Right, well, we ain't done bad by Drapers Alley. Over the years, when your brothers got hitched, I saw off the neighbours and a few more bungs to the council made sure the boys got their empty houses.' Dan leaned back in his chair, smiling with satisfaction. 'It's all Drapers living here now, other than your cousin Ivy, but she *was* a Draper before she married that short-arsed git.'

Chris had to grin. It was true. Ivy had married Steve Rawlings, a bloke whose head came up only to her shoulders. Mind, with her looks she was lucky to get anyone to take her on. Ivy was the odd one out and could only be described as ugly. She was tall, big built, with a round flat face, piggy little eyes and thin, mousy hair. The trouble was, Ivy had an ugly personality to match and Chris would never understand why his father had secured a house for her in the alley.

There was a clatter of footsteps as Petula ran downstairs before bursting into the room.

'Dad, can I have some money? Elvis Presley's latest record is in the charts and I want to buy it.'

'I gave you a quid yesterday!'

'Please, Dad,' she wheedled.

Chris knew that Pet would get her own way. She'd been born when he was ten, and had quickly become his father's pride and joy. At first he'd resented this, but gradually, like all his brothers, he had fallen under his baby sister's spell. She had been a beautiful child, and even though she was now a gangly fourteen-year-old, it was plain to see that she'd be stunning as an adult. Pet's hair was almost black, sitting on her shoulders and flicked into an outward curl at the ends. With vivid, blue eyes, a cute turned-up nose, full lips, and slightly pointed chin, her features were in perfect symmetry. Luckily, so far Pet seemed to have no idea how pretty she was.

Petula continued to beg and as usual, she won, Dan putting his hand in his back pocket to draw out a ten-shilling note. 'All right, but this is coming out of your pocket money.'

'Thanks, Dad,' she cried. 'I'll be back soon.'

'Hold on! Eat your breakfast first. I don't want you roaming around Clapham Junction on your own. Chris can go with you.'

'Dad,' she whined, 'I'm fourteen years old and I'll be fifteen in December. I can look after myself now.'

'You'll do as I say.'

Petula pouted, but her father's tone had hardened and she knew better than to argue further. She went into the kitchen, returning with a box of cornflakes. The pout was still there as she poured herself a bowl of the cereal, but she had a naturally light-hearted personality, and soon brightened when Chris winked at her.

'I want to buy a record too so I might as well come with you,' he said, his tone placatory.

Pet smiled, then turned to her father, saying, 'Dad, there's a dance at the youth club tonight. Can I go?'

'What time does it finish?'

'Ten o'clock.'

'Yeah, you can go, but one of your brothers will meet you afterwards to walk you home.'

'Oh, Dad, there's no need for that. It's less than fifteen minutes away. I'll be fine on my own.'

'You'll be met,' he insisted.

'None of my friends will be escorted home. I'll be a laughing stock.'

'It ain't safe for you to be wandering the streets at that time of night, so either you're met by one of your brothers, or you don't go.'

Pet scowled, saying no more as she quickly ate her breakfast. Chris finished his, and they got up from the table simultaneously.

'Right, we're off,' he said. 'See you later.'

'Yeah, and keep an eye out,' Dan warned. 'Don't forget we've got a meeting at the yard later. I want you there by eleven.'

'I'll be there. Bye, Mum.'

Joan obviously hadn't heard them, locked as usual in her own world, but nevertheless Chris still offered a small wave.

The weather was mild as they stepped out into the alley but, dwarfed by the factory wall, they felt the sun on their faces only as they turned into Aspen Street. Chris swiftly looked both ways, but other than a few kids playing there was no one in sight. Nowadays he knew it was unlikely that there'd be any trouble, but even so he was cautious. With the enemies they'd made it was sensible to be vigilant, but Petula's desire for more freedom was becoming a problem. They were supposed to be running a legitimate business so did their best to keep her in ignorance of why she needed protection, but he worried that it couldn't last much longer. Pet was growing up and they'd need to come up with some sort of explanation for her. He'd have a quiet word with his dad later, but in the meantime Chris continued to keep a lookout, more so when they traversed a few more streets and reached Lavender Hill.

Halfway along the hill, past the town hall, the police station loomed, and Chris gave a wry smile as he glanced at it. The Drapers were notorious in South London and had once been thieves, but careful planning had ensured they'd never been caught. It had been a long time since they'd done a job, but the last one they'd carried out had been close. Tipped off about a large consignment, they had cracked a jeweller's safe, and only just managed to get away. Of course, it helped that the entrance to the alley wasn't wide enough to accommodate a police car, but they'd been raided on foot, the rozzers pouring through the gaps at both ends of the alley. He grinned. Of course the police had found nothing then, and never had – the Draper family outfoxed them every time.

Pet broke into his thoughts. 'Look, there's Mrs Fuller.'

Chris saw the woman walking towards them, her mouth tightening as she drew closer. Nearly everyone knew their reputation and feared them, knowing better than to enter Drapers Alley without invitation. Some locals would come to them if they had a problem, and if Dan thought their complaint fair, he'd step in. His reputation was usually enough to put the shit up the troublemaker.

Betty Fuller was one of the exceptions. She had known Chris and Petula's father since they were both youngsters and felt it her right to enter the alley, although she did so rarely.

There was no fear on her face as she approached them. 'Watcha, Chris – Petula,' she said.

Chris merely nodded, but Petula said, 'Hello, Mrs Fuller.'

'How's your dad? Er . . . and your mum?' she added as an afterthought.

'They're fine, thanks.'

Chris knew that Betty Fuller was a gossip and he was anxious to get away, scowling when she said,

'Did you hear that someone done over the off-licence last night?'

'No,' Chris said shortly.

'Oh, so it was nothing to do with you lot then?'

Chris stiffened, annoyed at the woman's nerve *and* the innuendo. 'You must be joking. We run a legit business, and even if we didn't, we wouldn't be interested in a poxy off-licence. If I was you, Mrs Fuller, I'd nip that bit of gossip in the bud.'

The woman didn't pale at his implied threat. Instead she bristled, 'It didn't come from me – I'm only passing on what I heard.'

'Yeah, well, perhaps next time you hear any rubbish, you'll pass on that bit of info, *and* the fact that we won't be happy if we hear any more bad-mouthing.'

'I suppose I could do that.'

'Good. Come on, Pet,' Chris urged, taking his sister's arm and pulling her forward.

Pet was quiet for a few moments as they walked along, but then she said sadly, 'When are people going to stop talking about us?'

'Take no notice. The business is doing well and people are jealous because we've got a few bob. If anyone gets funny with you, let me know.'

'I'm a big girl now and can stick up for myself, but I don't understand why everyone still thinks that our family are criminals.'

'It's just gossip,' Chris said dismissively. 'Now come

13

on, let's get a move on. There's a business meeting at the yard today, and you heard Dad: he wants me there by eleven.'

As they picked up their pace, Chris hid a smile. Yes, they had become so-called legit, but it hadn't stopped CID from having a go at the yard. They'd wasted their time because all that was on show were building materials and perfectly kept account books. Drapers Builders' Merchants, the family business, was a good front and a cover that served them well. Chris hoped it would continue to do so, especially as nowadays they had a more lucrative sideline, one that was out of the borough and more likely to attract the attention of the Vice Squad. So far they'd been lucky, and had kept the business well concealed, but they were ruffling a few feathers so were always at risk from their rivals.

'What record are you buying?' Pet asked as they reached Clapham Junction. Chris's thoughts had been wandering, and he had just grunted in response to his sister's chatter so now he floundered for a reply. 'Er . . . "The Young Ones".'

'Not Cliff Richard and the Shadows?'

'Yeah, that's it.'

'Cliff Richard isn't bad-looking, but he isn't a patch on Elvis.'

'I'm not buying it for his looks. I rate his backing group, especially Hank Marvin on guitar.'

They turned into the entrance of Arding and

14

Hobbs, heading for the small record department at the back of the store. At nine thirty in the morning it was almost empty. Chris eyed the assistant, liking what he saw, and smiled as he and Pet approached the counter. It wasn't much fun being Pet's minder, but if this girl was available she'd be the ideal cover. She was young, pretty, and the sort of girlfriend his family would expect him to have on his arm.

Dan Draper eyed his wife as she bustled around. Joan was showing her age, but when he'd married her she'd been a stunner, a bundle of dynamite. Now, though, her hair was greying, her face lined, and the firm body he'd once gone mad for resembled a little round ball. Still, she'd been a good wife, keeping her mouth shut and not asking questions. As if aware of his scrutiny she met his eyes, her hand involuntarily patting her tightly permed hair.

'You spoil that girl,' she said.

'Leave it out, Queen. I only gave her ten bob.'

'Petula should earn it instead of having it dished out every time she bats her eyelashes at you.'

'Don't be daft, woman. She's only fourteen so how's she supposed to earn it?'

'For a start she could give me a hand around the house. It's about time she learned how to cook and clean.'

'The boys didn't have to earn their pocket money, so it shouldn't be any different for Petula.'

'They didn't get the amount of money you throw at her.'

Dan's lips tightened. He wasn't going to stand for this. Joan did all right; she had a large housekeeping allowance, giving her little to complain about. He treated her right, saw that the kids showed her respect, but he was the boss, the man of the house and she'd better remember that. 'If I want to treat my daughter now and again I will. Now for fuck's sake, shut up about it.'

Joan paled, but did as she was told, whilst Dan picked up the daily paper. He turned to the racing page, studying form before picking out a couple of bets. Nowadays he could afford to lay on a good few bob, and a satisfied expression crossed his features. Since they'd got into this new game, things had looked up big time. The money was still rolling in, and though at first he'd had reservations about getting into this line of work, he was glad that his sons had talked him round.

Yes, his dream was closer, but as he glanced at Joan he wondered how she'd fit into his planned new lifestyle. In the near future he was determined to retire – to hand the reins over to Danny junior, his eldest son. A nice house in Surrey beckoned, one with stables for the horses he intended to buy. Instead of a punter, he'd be an owner, mixing with the élite, looked up to and respected. Petula would love it and instead of hiding his wealth he would be able to dress her like a princess. She'd be away from this area and the riffraff, mixing instead with the upper echelons of the racing fraternity.

Joan went through to the kitchen and Dan heard the tap running, the clatter of plates as she washed up the breakfast dishes. Housework. All his wife thought about was housework. How the hell was she going to adapt to living in a big house, with cleaners paid to take over her role? Huh, Joan would probably insist on doing it herself, making a fool of them when they entertained. The trouble was, she had no class. Joan was a born-and-bred Battersea girl, and, unlike him, she had no interest in rising socially. He heaved a sigh. At least Petula would fit in. He'd made sure his daughter spoke well, paying for her to take elocution lessons from an old biddy in Chelsea. Yes, Petula could mix with the best so he'd just have to keep Joan and her working-class attitude in the background.

Dan rose to his feet, passing his wife to go through to the bathroom where he locked the door behind him. Involuntarily, as always, his eyes went straight to the hiding place. Joan cleaned in here every day, but had never discovered its secret. If she didn't twig it, then the police never would. Only the boys knew and he trusted them to keep their mouths shut, his married sons knowing better than to blab to their wives.

He washed and shaved before taking the money

he needed from the secret cache, returning to the living room with it tucked into his back pocket. 'Right, Queen, I'm off. I'm going down to the yard.'

Joan was busy as usual, and just nodded an acknowledgement when he left. As Dan stepped outside, he paused to look up and down Drapers Alley. It felt like his – his kingdom, and in some ways he'd regret leaving it. He patted the money in his back pocket and did a mental calculation. The cash was for stock, more bricks and cement, enough to keep the yard ticking over, but there'd be enough left to place a few bets. The other business was thriving and maybe they'd have to increase productivity to keep up with the demand. It was lucrative, but with five sons and Ivy's husband wanting their share, they needed to push harder.

Dan passed through the narrow entrance, deciding to buy some cigarettes before going to the lockup where he kept his car. He walked the length of Aspen Street, and as he went into the corner shop, two customers moved swiftly to one side. He smiled tightly, taking their obvious fear and respect as his right.

'Morning, Bill. Twenty Senior Service, please.'

Bill Tweedy was showing his age nowadays, his hairline receding whilst his waistline widened. 'Morning, Dan, coming up,' he said, taking the cigarettes from a shelf behind him and laying them on the counter. 'I suppose you've heard that the off-licence was done over last night? I hope I'm not next.'

'No, it's news to me,' Dan said, frowning with annoyance. The off-licence was just round the corner, in his territory. If he found out who the toerags were he'd have their guts for garters. 'Any word on who did it?'

'Nah, but if I get wind of anything I'll let you know.'

'Yeah, do that, and don't worry, I'll sort them out,' he said, paying for the cigarettes.

Dan was still seething as he walked out of the shop. Over the years he had made sure that the area surrounding Drapers Alley was out of bounds to petty criminals. Local businesses, along with the residents, feared him, but were glad of his protection, and if the police asked questions they knew it was wise to keep their mouths shut. Now it seemed that someone was trying it on and would need sorting out. He'd put his boys on to it, but for now, as Dan climbed into his Daimler, he dismissed it from his mind.

There was a powwow today as his eldest son, Danny, had come up with a way to increase the coffers. Dan grimaced, thinking about the rough plan his son had outlined. He felt it too risky, but would wait to gauge his other sons' reactions before vetoing the idea.

For a moment Dan smiled, knowing that if he

voted against Danny's plans, his other sons would follow suit, all bending to his will. If Joan knew what they were up to she'd have a fit, but there was no chance of her finding out. How the daft cow thought the builders' merchants made enough money to support them all was beyond him, but as long as she carried on living in a world of illusions, that was fine by him.

Chapter Two

Next door, in number two Drapers Alley, the eldest son, Danny junior, emerged from the bedroom. His dark hair was tousled and his mouth open in a wide yawn, but even this couldn't detract from his looks. Danny was handsome, a six-foot-two charmer with large, sultry dark eyes and full lips. A long, thin scar on his cheek, the relic of a knife fight, didn't scare off women. If anything the scar added a hint of danger that complemented his rakish charms.

'Why didn't you wake me?' he moaned as he walked into the kitchen.

His wife, Yvonne, pouring him a cup of tea, said shortly, 'I didn't know you had to get up for work today.'

His eyes darkened with anger – he was certain he'd told her there was going to be a business meeting that morning. 'Shit, I'm sure I mentioned it. If I don't get a move on the old man will arrive before me.'

Yvonne pushed the cup of tea towards him, her hazel eyes avoiding his. She was tall, her height emphasised by the pencil skirt she was wearing with a crisp, white blouse tucked in at the waist. Her shoulder-length brown hair was immaculate as usual, and her make-up freshly applied. When Danny first met Yvonne she had reminded him of Wallis Simpson, with the same elegant manner and style of dress. However, unlike the sophisticated woman who had captured a king, Yvonne showed her true class as soon as she opened her mouth. Like his mother, she was Battersea born and bred, her diction letting her down and sometimes grating on his nerves. Even so, he'd been instantly smitten. But as the years passed she'd grown so thin that the woman he'd once been attracted to now resembled a stick insect. Yvonne's jumpiness was generally put down to her suffering with her nerves, but he knew the real problem. The skinny cow wanted a kid, but even though they'd been trying for seven years, it seemed she was barren. Not that it bothered him. As far as he was concerned his life was fine without brats cramping his style. Of course, Yvonne didn't know that; the daft mare thought he was as keen on the idea of a family as she was.

Danny gulped the tea before hurrying through to the bathroom. He had to get a move on or his father might talk to the others before he arrived, putting the kibosh on his ideas. After running water into the sink he cupped some in his hands to splash on his face, decided to forgo a shave, but still smacked some Brut aftershave onto his cheeks. It was a big day today. He hoped his brothers would back his plans but maybe he should have approached them individually first. Danny cursed his lack of forethought. Yet surely his brothers would see the sense of it, and if the old man wasn't keen, maybe they'd go against him for once. Yes, there'd be risks, big ones, but the rewards could be vast – a way out of Drapers Alley for all of them.

He returned to the kitchen, drank a ready-poured second cup of tea, and held a slice of toast between his teeth as he tucked his shirt into his trousers.

'See you later,' he called as he left the room without a backward glance.

Yvonne's eyes followed Danny. There was no kiss goodbye, no quick hug of affection, and as the street door slammed behind him, desolately she went upstairs.

In the bedroom she picked up the shirt that Danny had discarded when he rolled home after midnight, and lifted it to her nose. It reeked of cheap perfume, confirming her suspicions that Danny was playing away again. Tears stung her eyes. How many affairs had she put up with? Yvonne had lost count, but each time he'd assured her it would be the last. She was a fool, a mug, an idiot for believing him, but she loved Danny so deeply and couldn't bear to leave him.

Oh, if only they'd had children. She knew Danny resented it, knew that he envied his married brothers with small families, whilst they remained childless. He blamed her, of course, said she was barren and he was right. Maybe that was why he kept having affairs. Maybe if he got another woman pregnant, he'd leave her! Yvonne slumped onto the side of the bed, tears rolling down her cheeks.

Ten minutes passed before Yvonne was able to pull herself together. She then rose to her feet, throwing the shirt into the laundry basket. She had to get a move on – had to make sure everything was clean and tidy in case her mother-in-law popped round. Joan had high standards, ones that Yvonne, always looking for her mother-in-law's approval, fought to match.

She made the bed, and though it was unlikely that Joan would see it, Yvonne ensured the sheets were tucked in with tight hospital corners, plumped the pillows and shook out the pale blue quilt. She then dusted the furniture and aligned the brush set on her dressing table in perfect symmetry.

A glance in the mirror showed her red, puffy eyes. Fearful that Joan would see them, Yvonne ran downstairs to the bathroom to splash her face with cold water. Danny had left a mess, which she quickly tidied up, folding the discarded towel before placing it neatly on the rail. Like Joan's, this bathroom was an extension, added shortly after she married Danny, and Yvonne was proud of it. After her parents' outside toilet and tin bath in front of the fire every Friday night, having a proper bathroom was sheer luxury. Her eyes saddened. She still missed her mother, mourned her death after a long fight with cancer, and couldn't remember the last time she'd seen her father. He had disapproved of Danny, and had forced her to choose between them. It had nearly broken her heart but she couldn't give Danny up – yet as an only child, she had found losing her father hard to bear.

Half an hour later, the kitchen and living room were looking immaculate when there was a rap on the letter box. The door opened and Joan poked her head inside to call, 'It's only me.'

'Come in, Mum. I'm in the kitchen,' Yvonne called back as she arranged her best porcelain cups and saucers. No thick cheap pot for Joan. Carefully pouring the boiling water into the matching teapot, Yvonne plastered a smile on her face as her mother-in-law walked in.

But there was no fooling Joan Draper. 'Have you been crying?'

'No, of course not,' Yvonne quickly protested, knowing that Danny would go mad if she complained to his mother. Quickly finding an excuse she stammered, 'I . . . I've got a bit of a cold, that's all.'

'You want to look after it or it could turn into bronchitis.'

Why anyone would want to look after a cold was beyond Yvonne, but then a lot of the things that Joan came out with sounded daft to her. They weren't religious, but Joan insisted on eating fish on Fridays, and the routine of housework was the same: washing on Monday, rain or shine; ironing on Tuesday; in fact every day had its own designated task. The woman was like a little beaver, always busy doing something, so it was a wonder she took time out every day to come round for a cup of tea. Yvonne found her mother-in-law a bit of a Jekyll and Hyde character: meek when her husband was around, but made of sterner stuff when he wasn't.

'Do you fancy digestive or Garibaldi biscuits?' she asked.

'Digestive, please,' Joan said, but then her lips tightened. 'Chris has taken Pet to Clapham Junction. Dan gave her the money to buy a record, but I wish he'd stop spoiling the girl.'

Yvonne knew that her mother-in-law was wishing for the moon. Dan Draper was a hard man, and despite the fact that his sons were adults, he still ruled them all. Only Petula saw his soft side, and it was true, the girl *was* spoiled. Thankfully, it hadn't ruined her character so far, but she'd be ill prepared if she ever had to face the real world. Petula had been cosseted and sheltered since the day she was born, wanting for nothing. Mind, it wasn't only her father who treated her like a little princess. Her brothers were just as bad, all of them over-protective when it came to their little sister.

Joan's eyes flicked around the small kitchen but it didn't worry Yvonne. Every surface was shiny and clean, everything in its rightful place, and her mother-in-law would be unable to find fault. Yvonne picked up the prettily laid tray, carrying it through to the sitting room where they sat at the table.

Joan hated tea leaves in her drink, so Yvonne poured carefully, holding a strainer over the cups. She then added milk from a matching jug, a spoonful of sugar from a matching bowl, and handed it to her mother-in-law.

'Thanks,' Joan said, then added abruptly, 'Linda's pregnant.'

Yvonne stiffened. Linda had married Danny's brother, George, less than a year ago and they now lived in number five. He was her least favourite brother-in-law, quick to violence, but she couldn't help a surge of envy. They'd been married for such a short time but already had a baby on the way. Oh God, it just wasn't fair. She struggled to pull herself together, forcing a smile. 'That's nice, but is it defin-ite? She hasn't said anything to me.'

There was a pause as Joan lifted the cup to drink

her tea. She then said, 'Linda knows it's a sensitive subject so maybe she doesn't want to hurt your feelings.'

'Once she starts showing, she can hardly hide it.'

'Yeah, that's true. Oh, well, I suppose I'll have to get my knitting needles out again. This will be my fourth grandchild, but it's been a while since I've had to make any matinée jackets.'

Yvonne felt a wave of desolation. It was as though her mother-in-law enjoyed rubbing salt into the wound – but why? She tried to be a good wife, kept the house spotless, and though she and Danny remained childless, Joan had other grandchildren to love. Huh, love – that was a joke. When did Joan ever show any of her grandchildren an ounce of affection?

Yvonne shook her head, unable to help herself from saying sadly, 'I envy Linda. I want a baby more than anything in the world.'

Joan leaned forward to pat the back of Yvonne's hand, saying softly, 'I know you do, love. Don't worry, it might still happen.'

Yvonne blinked wildly to stave off the tears welling in her eyes, but Joan rose to her feet, saying hurriedly, 'I'd best be off. Thanks for the tea.'

Before Yvonne could respond, Joan had gone, and she was left sitting at the table, amazed that her usually cold, undemonstrative mother-in-law had actually shown her a little sympathy.

*   *   *

Joan almost ran into her front door, closing it quickly behind her. Gawd, she had almost brought Yvonne to tears and that was the last thing she wanted. Of all her daughters-in-law, Yvonne was the only one she had any time for, and she could guess the sort of life Danny led the poor girl.

Joan wasn't a fool, she knew Danny's faults and it was a wonder he'd managed to hold on to Yvonne for seven years. He was a womaniser, but if his father found out he'd go mad. Joan also knew that Yvonne longed for children, but was tempted to tell her what a thankless task motherhood was. She had hoped that after five sons, things would be different with Petula, but like the boys, she favoured her father. Maybe things would have been different if she could have shown them affection, but Joan found it impossible. Her own mother had been a cold, unloving woman, bitter at being a single parent with the stigma it carried.

With a sigh, Joan picked up a duster, absent-mindedly flicking it over furniture she'd already polished. Her mother had been a dirty woman, their home a tip, and they'd been looked down on by their neighbours. During her infrequent attendance at school, Joan had been called a smelly cow and at first she hadn't understood why. It was only as she grew older that she learned about hygiene – learned that her mother's method of rubbing a damp flannel across her face every day, leaving her body untouched, wasn't enough. Her first bath had been a revelation – the water almost black – but from then on she had gone to the public baths once a week, relishing the feel of being clean from top to toe.

She'd known that Dan was a bit of a rogue when she met him but, as he always had a few bob in his pocket, she chose to ignore the gossip. He would buy her presents, make her laugh and she found herself falling in love. When he proposed she had quickly said yes, eager to get away from the dour life she had lived with her mother.

When they moved into their first tiny flat, Joan had been determined to be different, to make sure that her home was always immaculate. At first it had been easy, but as the babies came along it took every minute of her day to keep up. Then, just when she thought her child-bearing days were over, Petula had been born. Though she hated to admit it, Joan had been filled with resentment. She'd had enough of babies, dirty nappies, broken sleep – but she'd hidden her feelings and left most of Petula's welfare to her father and older brothers. That had been a mistake. Petula was fawned on, indulged, but it was too late to change things now. If Joan so much as opened her mouth in criticism, Danny shot her down in flames. His precious daughter was able to do no wrong.

'We're back,' Chris said, flinging open the door. 'I can't stop. Dad wants me down the yard.'

'I thought it was your Saturday off,' Joan said.

Chris looked surprised at her interest. 'Yeah, but there's some sort of business meeting and Dad wants me there.'

'It's the first I've heard of it.'

'He mentioned it earlier. You obviously weren't listening.'

'What's this meeting about?'

Chris's eyes became veiled and Joan knew she was wasting her time. She was always kept in the dark when it came to the business. In truth, she preferred it that way, and berated herself now for asking questions.

'I'm not sure what it's about, Mum, but no doubt Dad will put you in the picture.'

'Yeah, and pigs might fly,' Joan told him.

He grinned, turning to leave. 'See you later, Mum. Bye, Petula.'

'Don't call me Petula. You know I hate it.'

'It was Mum who named you after Petula Clark, who was a child star before you were born, so don't blame me.' On that note, Chris closed the street door behind him.

'It's a daft name,' Petula complained.

Joan ignored her daughter and went through to the kitchen to boil a kettle of water. She would scrub the doorstep before getting the Brasso out to polish the letter box and door knocker. With any luck it might inspire her daughters-in-law to follow suit. Yvonne was the only one who had good standards. The rest were slovenly, and it was about time they pulled their socks up.

She heard Petula thumping up the stairs, followed by the sound of her new record filling the house. Her youngest was growing up, and no doubt she was already interested in boys. Not that she'd have much luck meeting any, especially with her father and brothers keeping her under close guard. The day would come when Petula would rebel, and for the first time Joan felt a twinge of pity for her daughter. The girl would be fighting a losing battle. Any man who came near her would soon be chased off.

By the time the kettle came to the boil, Petula was playing the song again, and Joan closed her eyes against the sound. Every time the girl got a new record it was played repeatedly until Joan felt like screaming. All right, Elvis Presley had a good voice, but by now she knew all his songs off by heart. Her ears pricked. What was this one? 'Good Luck Charm'. Well, it wasn't bad, but Joan decided to get away from the racket. She took a bucket of hot water and soda outside to tackle her doorstep.

'All right, Mum?' a voice called, and Joan's eyes flicked sideways.

Sue was standing on her doorstep, the third house in the row, and Joan hid a scowl. This was her least favourite daughter-in-law. Like her, Sue was diminutive, but the resemblance ended there. With